WELCOME TO THE WORLD OF Geronimo Stilton

GERONIMO
STILTON

Published by Sweet Cherry Publishing Limited
Unit 36, Vulcan House,
Vulcan Road,
Leicester, LE5 3EF,
United Kingdom

First published in the UK in 2018
2018 edition

ISBN: 978-1-78226-371-5

Text by Geronimo Stilton
Art Director: Iacopo Bruno
Graphic Designer: Laura Dal Maso / theWorldofDOT
Original cover illustration by Roberto Ronchi and Christian Aliprandi
Concept of illustration by Roberta Bianchi, produced by Alessandro Pastrovicchio with the assistance of Lara Martinelli and Tommaso Valsecchi
Initial and final page illustrations by Roberto Ronchi and Ennio Bufi MAD5, Studio Parlapà and Andrea Cavallini. Map illustrations by Andrea Da Rold and Andrea Cavallini
Cover layout and typography by Elena Distefano
Interior layout and typography by Cecilia Bennett, Rhiannon Izard and Amy Wong
Graphics by Yuko Egusa

Original title: *Ore 8: a scuola di formaggio!*
Based on an original idea by Elisabetta Dami

www.geronimostilton.com/uk

www.sweetcherrypublishing.com

Printed and bound in Turkey

Geronimo Stilton

A FANTASTIC SCHOOL ADVENTURE

Sweet Cherry
Publishing

A Very Special Morning

It's true. **I am not a morning mouse.** But one autumn day, things got off to an especially bad start. Maybe it was because my alarm clock went off too early, or because I had to skip breakfast. Then again, maybe it was because I was in a **MAD RUSH**. That morning just started off on the wrong paw: it was a typical bad day. You know what I mean. It was one of those days

when anything that could go wrong did go wrong.

I'm the kind of mouse who likes routine. In the morning, I wake up **s l o w l y**, stretch **l a z i l y** and cuddle back under my covers, and lounge for a while. I like to pick out my clothes carefully and then eat a hearty, leisurely breakfast before I leave for work.

I'm not the kind of mouse who **JUMPS** out of bed at the crack of dawn and immediately starts doing yoga. No way!

As I was saying, that morning things seemed to be **extra topsy-turvy**.

First, the alarm went off extra early. It rang at 6:30 a.m., an hour before I usually get up! I stretched my arm, turned it off, and turned over to catch a

few more ZZZs. I couldn't even think about getting up. **It was just too early.** But I knew I had to force myself out of bed, because it was a very special day for my nephew Benjamin! It was **Career Day** at his school, and I had been invited to be a GUEST SPEAKER. On **Career Day**, different people come in to talk about their jobs, and I was going to tell Benjamin's class about mine.

Oops, I'm sorry. I haven't told you what I do. I'm a writer, editor, and publisher. I publish the most famouse newspaper on Mouse Island, *The Rodent's Gazette*.

Everybody in New Mouse City reads it! My name is Stilton, *Geronimo Stilton.*

If you want to know the truth, the thought of speaking in front of Benjamin's friends, his teachers, and the other guests made my tail quiver. It made my whiskers shaky and my paws soggy with sweat. I'm a very shy mouse and I get terrible stage fright when I have to speak in front of people. I stammer and mix up words. I become clumsy. I get so **FRAZZLED** I usually make a fool of myself! Nevertheless, I knew it was a very special day for Benjamin. I'd jump though flaming hoops for my nephew! I had to be super cool and smart, too.

"I'll make Benjamin proud!"

I'M NOT A MORNING MOUSE!

I was already stressed out about my speech. To ease my nerves, I took a deep breath and repeated these words: *I will not embarrass Benjamin. I am a smart, successful mouse.*

I was starting to relax when the phone rang. I jumped up to answer it and bumped my head on the shelf over my bed.

OUCH! What a nasty wake-up call!

I answered the phone. It was my sister Thea.

"Geronimo, you're still in bed, aren't you?" she said. "Hurry up! Don't you remember what day it is? Please, try not to look like a **FOOL** in front of everybody. Benjamin looks up to you!"

"I'm awake (almost)," I muttered. "And of course I remember what day it is! Don't worry. I have no intention of looking like a **FOOL** (but I usually end up looking like one anyway)."

I hung up the phone and sighed. Now I was nervous all over again! I repeated my mousetra* aloud: "I WILL NOT EMBARRASS BENJAMIN. I AM A SMART, SUCCESSFUL MOUSE."

When I finally found the oomph to get up,

*A MOUSETRA, LIKE A MANTRA, IS A PHRASE THAT YOU REPEAT TO GIVE YOURSELF COMFORT OR CONFIDENCE it was 6:50 a.m. I had to move like a mouse in a rat race! That's when my mobile phone rang. It was Grandfather William.

"Geronimo! Are you ready?" he asked. "You're not going to be late, are you? Of all days, not today! And I beg you, please don't make a **FOOL** of yourself. Benjamin really looks up to you! And above all, remember: the family's good name is at stake here, as well as that of The Rodent's Gazette."

My whiskers got all in a knot just listening to him.

"Of course, Grandfather," I answered. "I know Benjamin looks up to me."

I tried to cut him off, but he went on and on for a full ten minutes! I had just hung up when the doorbell rang. It was Aunt Sweetfur.

"Good morning, Geronimo," she said. "I was just passing by and thought I'd stop in to say hello. I hope it's not a bad time."

"Thank you, Aunt Sweetfur," I replied. "No, you're not bothering me at all. Come right in."

"I brought you something sweet to give you a little courage. I know how hard it is for you to talk in front of a crowd. But, please, try to do your very best. Benjamin looks up to you!"

"It's always a pleasure talking with you, Aunt Sweetfur, and your goodies are such a treat," I told her.

She stayed for ten minutes, which was enough time to leave me **Cheesecake cookies**, a warm smile, and a couple of tips.

I was looking forward to savouring a rich and creamy cookie when I got a text message.

It was from Petunia Pretty Paws.

Hi, G. Break a leg today. Benjamin looks up to you. See you soon.

Wow, Petunia was so sweet to text me. And she had written **"See you soon!"**

Hmm, could it mean maybe, just maybe, she wanted to see me?

With my head

swirling in the clouds, I began *daydreaming* about her. I started to text Petunia back, but my paws were all clammy. Just thinking about her made my fingers feel like jelly. When I looked down to see what I had typed, it was all a **JUMBLE**.

I had wanted to write: "Thanks, I hope to see you soon, too," but I was so jittery, my fingers kept slipping on the keys. I went to erase the message, but accidentally punched the SEND button! What bad luck. **Why me?**

Then the doorbell rang again. This time it was Trap! He whipped into the house like a **Tasmanian devil**!

"Gerry, Gerry, quite contrary, why aren't you ready?" Trap asked. "You know whenever you have to hurry, you get all **FRAZZLED**. And then you end up having a bad day."

"If you would leave me alone so I could get ready, I wouldn't have to rush," I said.

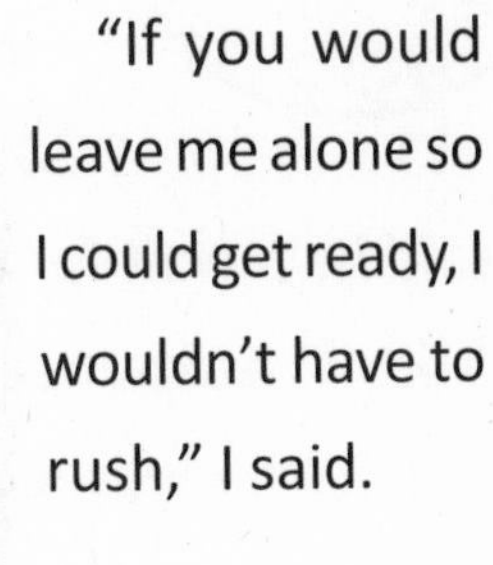

"Are you nervous?" he asked.

"No, I'm not nervous."

"See. You *are* nervous. It's a bad case of jitters, I tell you."

"I said no, I'm not nervous."

"Are you sure?" Trap prodded. "Because when you get nervous, you always make a **FOOL** of yourself."

"I'm not nervous! But if you don't let me get ready, I'm going to –"

"Calm down," Trap said. "I told you, you're nervous. Just try to relax, or we're all going to end up looking silly."

"ENOOOUGH, I GET IT!"

I screeched.

When I finally got rid of Trap, it was 7:50 a.m. Now I really *was* late! Benjamin said he'd wait for me at his school bus stop at 8 a.m. **Yikes!** I wasn't ready and had run out of time!

I quickly washed my face, dressed, and ran outside

... without eating my breakfast!

It was definitely turning out to be a bad day!

DEFINITELY A BAD DAY

The alarm clock went off too early: at 6:30 a.m.!

When the phone rang, I was startled and hit my head on the bookshelf.

Aunt Sweetfur brought me some whisker-licking good cookies that I didn't have time to eat!

Luckily, I got a text message from my friend Petunia Pretty Paws!

Trap stormed in and made me even more nervous than before!

THANKS, I PREFER GETTING CARSICK

I got to the bus stop just in the nick of time. As soon as Benjamin saw me, he gave me a **HIGH FIVE** that made my paw sting! He was so excited that I almost forgot that I was a having a bad day. I even forgot that I hadn't eaten breakfast!

He grabbed my jacket, dragged me to the back of the bus, and sat me down in his favourite seat in the very last row. When I was a little mouseling, I could never sit in the back of the bus: I THREW UP EVERY TIME I TRIED!

But I didn't say anything to Benjamin: I wanted the day to be **VERY SPECIAL** for him. I couldn't let him down! So I sat in the back of the bus and crossed my whiskers that I wouldn't get sick. Unfortunately, my stomach was as empty as a cookie jar after a mouseling birthday party, and I always get queasy when I'm hungry.

In fact, as soon as the bus took off bumping and thumping, my stomach started **SLOSHING**.

After the first curve, I was as white as a ghost.

After the second curve, I was as green as pistachio ice cream.

After the third curve, I felt dismally dizzy.

What a ghastly ride!

Then the bus hit a pothole, and a loose spring in the seat poked me right in the tail. I yelped and jumped up, landing two rows up, right in between a cute pigtailed mouseling and a freckle-faced mouseling. I was wedged between them like a slice of Cheddar on a grilled cheese sandwich. Their squeaky voices poked holes right through my eardrums.

What a ghastly ride!

"Are you Stilton, *Geronimo Stilton*?" the freckle-faced mouseling asked.

"Is it really you?" asked the pigtailed mouseling.

"Is it really, really you? Are you the one who writes all those books?"

I smiled, pleased with myself.

"Of course it's me!" I insisted.

"Good," the boy mouseling said. "I wanted to tell you that on PAGE TWENTY-SEVEN of your last book, there is a mistake in the SEVENTH WORD on the FIFTEENTH LINE. You spelled 'cheese' with only one 'e'! I'm surprised – I never expected it from you!"

The girl mouseling had to have her say as well. "It's true! I saw it, too! My aunt is best friends with Sally

Ratmousen's hairdresser's sister, and she said that Sally said that it was just SCANDALOUS!"

Hmph. Sally Ratmousen was the publisher of **The Daily Rat**, my paper's competitor. Leave it to her to be catty. I tried to change the subject, but the mouselings would not stop. I can't stand gossip!

What a ghastly trip!

Luckily, Benjamin came to my rescue.

"Come on, Uncle Geronimo," he said. "I want to introduce you to my friends."

I was about to follow him to our seat in the back of the bus when the two mouselings stopped me.

"Stay here, Mr. Stilton," they said. "If you sit in the back, you might throw up. You know who told me that you get carsick? My neighbour's sister's ..."

I felt my stomach GRUMBLE and GROWL. I wondered if I should stay with the two gossipy, catty, extra-chatty mouselings.

I decided I would rather get carsick!

"GERONIMO STILTON ..." "PRESENT!"

I took a seat at the back of the bus, hoping I wouldn't feel queasy again.

"Hang on, Uncle Geronimo," Benjamin reassured me. **"We're almost there!"**

The trip seemed endless.

A curve to the left ... A curve to the right ...

BANG! BANG! BANG!

The school bus did another three curves to the right and four curves to the left. A couple of **beastly bumps** made me hit my head on the roof! In the meantime, Benjamin was busy showing me the schedule for the morning at Little Tails Academy. I couldn't bear to look at it: **I was woefully woozy!** (I always get sick when I read on a moving vehicle.)

Here, read it yourselves:

	MON	TUE	WED	THU	FRI
8:30AM	Science	English	Reading	Reading	Science
10:30AM	Maths	Science	Maths	Gym	English
LUNCH					
1:30PM	Gym	Reading	Music	Maths	Maths
2:30PM	Art	History	History	Library	History

When I finally got off the bus, my head was spinning as if I had just got off the tallest, **MOST RICKETY** roller coaster of all time.

There was no doubt, it was a bad day.

I stumbled towards school. As soon as I stepped through the doors, a thousand memories came flooding back.

They were such happy memories!

I learned so much! I got into so much mischief! I made so many friends: Hercule Poirat, my detective friend; Kornelius von Kickpaw (he's Secret Agent 00K, but don't tell anyone!); and, obviously, my joke-loving cousin Trap.

And then there was *Veronica Stiffwhiskers*, my sworn enemy at Little Tails Academy. She was such a cute rodent, perfect in every way, and good at everything. **TOO GOOD.** The school had never seen such rivals as the two of us. We competed in everything, and she always won.

I stopped in front of the school's display case. I looked at all the students' plaques, medals, and trophies. Her name was everywhere. *Veronica Stiffwhiskers, Veronica Stiffwhiskers, Veronica Stiffwhiskers.*

She won the maths challenge, the spelling competition,

the essay contest, and I always got second prize. Second prize wasn't that bad, but I would have loved to be **NUMERO UNO** just once!

For years, I dreamed of having my name on a plaque or trophy in that display case. I sighed and walked away, feeling a little sad. I tried to console myself that, in spite of being number two, I had done quite well for myself: I'm the editor-in-chief and publisher of a newspaper, I have lots of friends, and I even won the RATITZER PRIZE. Despite all that, though, I still would have liked to see my name inside that case.

While these thoughts were rumbling through my head, Benjamin led me through the halls to his classroom.

The school had changed so much!

It was the same, but very different.

It was more modern: it had a computer lab, a new gym, language and music labs, an auditorium, and a *spectacular* art room. **Everything was state of the art!**

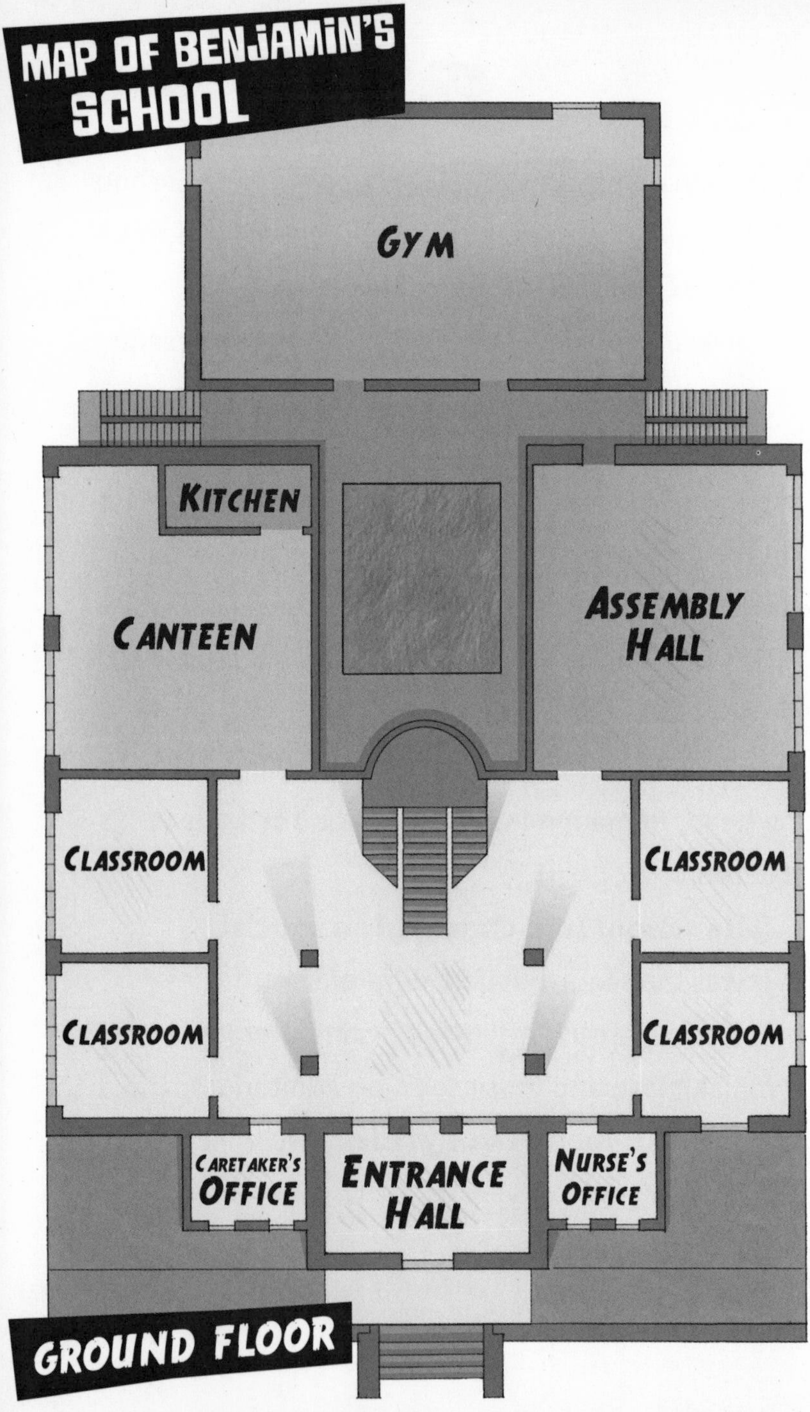

MAP OF BENJAMIN'S SCHOOL

GYM

KITCHEN

CANTEEN

ASSEMBLY HALL

CLASSROOM

CLASSROOM

CLASSROOM

CLASSROOM

CARETAKER'S OFFICE

ENTRANCE HALL

NURSE'S OFFICE

GROUND FLOOR

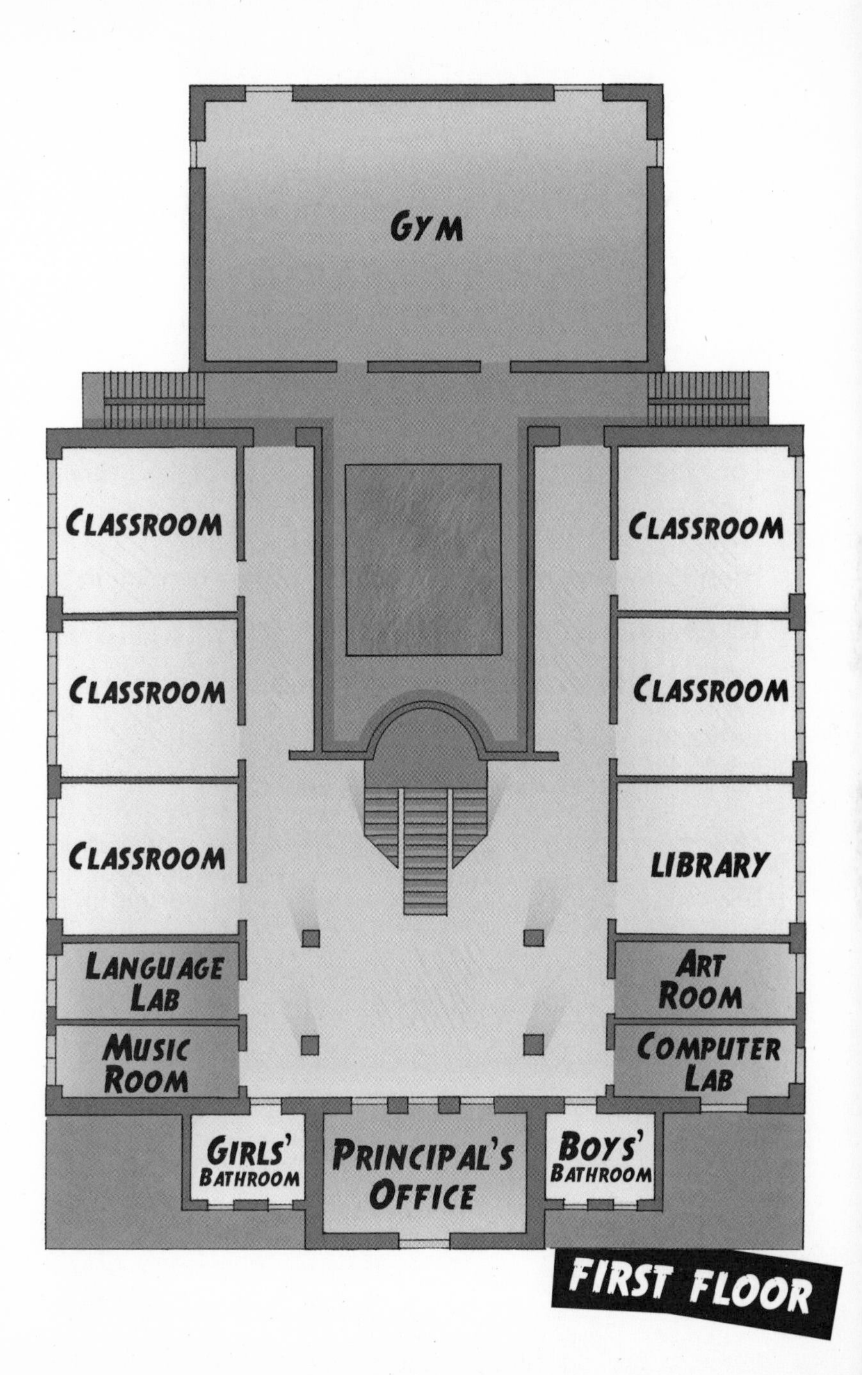
Gym
Classroom
Classroom
Classroom
Classroom
Classroom
Library
Language Lab
Art Room
Music Room
Computer Lab
Girls' Bathroom
Principal's Office
Boys' Bathroom
First Floor

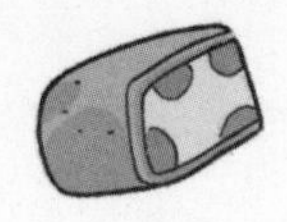

Like Mice in a Cheese Factory!

Looking at all those rooms, I longed for the days when I scampered along those halls with my friends. We had such adventures, like little mice in a **big cheese factory**!

But I didn't have any time to revel in my memories. Benjamin was pushing me into his classroom.

"Here we are, Uncle Geronimo!"

A rodent with long blonde hair and blue eyes came towards me. It was *Miss Angel Paws*, Benjamin's teacher.

She greeted me with a bright smile.

"Mr. Stilton, it's such a pleasure to have you with us today!" she exclaimed.

"Good morning, Miss Angel Paws," I replied as I reached out to shake her paw. "Thank you for inviting me.

It's a pleasure to see you again. And a good morning to you, class!"

I looked around and recognised the smiling faces of Benjamin's friends.

I knew them all because we had taken a ratastic field trip to **NIAGARA FALLS** together.

It felt good to be with the class, and I was starting to think that maybe my luck had changed when a voice came over the loudspeaker.

Miss Angel Paws!

Pssst!
Hello!
Good morning!
Hi!

"Miss Angel Paws, please come to the principal's office immediately."

The voice sounded very familiar, but I couldn't figure out why. Miss Angel Paws smiled at me.

"Geronimo, I'm leaving you in charge," she said. "Would you please do the register? If I don't come back within a few minutes, please take the students to the playground. Today our class is scheduled to raise the school flag: it's a **REAL HONOUR**. Oh, and Spike, our class pet, needs to be fed. That's about it. Is everything clear?"

I never say no to someone in need, so I nodded confidently.

"Don't worry," I said gallantly. "I'll take care of everything!"

As soon as the words came out of my mouth, I regretted them. I didn't have a clue how to lead a class. I had never done the register. I didn't know how to raise the flag.

I couldn't remember who was who. And, I was afraid to ask: what was Spike?

It was too late. **She was gone, and I was left to deal with things.**

Like a Flag in the Wind

I decided to start with the register.

I found the list of names and began to read them in alphabetical order: "Antonia."

"Here!"

"Benjamin."

"Uncle Geronimo, you know I'm here," he giggled. "You brought me to school! **Of course I'm here!**"

Everybody laughed and I turned as red as my tie. I quickly cleared my throat and tried to move on.

"Ahem, good. I wanted to make sure you were paying attention."

I went ahead with the rest of the register. Everything went well until **LATE IN THE ALPHABET**.

"Malcolm."

"Here!"

"Mohamed."

"Here!"

"Oliver."

"Here!"

"Punk Rat."

"Absent."

"What do you mean, absent?" I asked. "I recognise you from our field trip. You're **PUNK RAT**! I remember you."

In fact, I remembered him a little too well. How could I forget him?

During our trip to **NIAGARA FALLS**, he got into all kinds of trouble. And he blamed me!

"No, I'm not Punk Rat," he replied. "I'm his twin brother!"

"Don't try to fool me, **PUNK RAT**."

"I told you. I'm not Punk Rat. I'm his twin, Modest Mouse. We decided to switch schools for the day."

Everybody laughed, and I became **BRIGHT RED** all over again. Nevertheless, I decided to play along with his game.

"Okay, Modest Mouse, I'll write your name in the register. Punk Rat is absent. Modest Mouse is present. So, Modest Mouse, since you are our newest student, you will have the **HONOUR** of raising the flag. Do you think you can do that?" I asked.

"Of course I can," he replied. "I can do anything. I'm the type of mouse who likes to help out. Raising a flag is easy. Every mouse scout knows how to do it, unless he or she is so old that he or she has forgotten."

Everybody laughed, and I became redder than ever because it was true. **I couldn't remember how to raise a flag!** And even though Modest Mouse seemed to be acting nice, I had a feeling Punk Rat had a trick up his tail.

"Why, oh why, won't the teacher come back?" I muttered to myself as I tried to get the class under control again.

I finished the register without another mishap and then I took the class outside. We made a circle around the flagpole and got ready to raise the flag. I became very confused as I watched Punk Rat fumble with the hooks and pulley. I couldn't figure it out. The next thing I knew, Punk Rat pulled on the cord. As the flag went up the pole, I went right along with it!

I was waving like a flag in the wind!

"Help! Can somebody get me down from here?" I shouted. "I'm afraid of heights!"

The caretaker came running out. He looked very worried. "Hang in there, Mr. Stilton!"

He immediately pulled me down.

"Are you okay, Mr. Stilton?" he asked. "It's such an honour to meet you. I'm glad you flagged me down."

Hearing that word, I blushed again.

"Um, sorry," he said.

WHERE'S SPIKE?

I looked at the caretaker's calm face, brown eyes, and kind, wide smile.

His face seemed very familiar to me, as if I had known him all my life.

"Do we know each other?" I asked.

He smiled. "No, you don't know me, but I know all about you," he replied. "I'm **HENRY HANDIPAWS**, the caretaker here."

"Well, thank you for all your help," I said. "You really saved me, Mr. Handipaws."

I turned to face Punk Rat. "PUNK RAT, WE NEED TO HAVE A CHAT," I said sternly.

He looked at me innocently with his wide brown eyes.

"I'm not Punk Rat," he claimed. "Punk Rat is absent. I'm Modest Mouse, his twin. I'm a good mouse. I didn't do it on purpose."

I didn't have proof, but I was certain the little rodent had his paws all over the **flag fiasco**.

Anyway, I knew we should get back to the classroom. We still needed to feed Spike, and I wanted to make a good impression on Benjamin's teacher. As soon as we entered the room, Antonia came forwards. She had a PROUD SMILE on her snout.

"Today is my turn to feed Spike," she said

"Good. Why don't you take care of it right away?" I suggested. "By the way, what kind of animal is Spike?"

There was no need for anyone to tell me. **Unfortunately, I found out all by myself!**

As soon as Antonia opened the terrarium, something leaped out at lightning speed.

Everyone screeched as Spike, **TERRIFIED** by the students' screams, sped across the classroom floor. Spike **ZIGZAGGED**

under the desks, circled the cubbyholes, and then ran straight up my trouser leg, climbed under my vest, and popped out of my collar!

I gasped in surprise. **Spike was a scaly green gecko!**

ALL ABOUT GECKOS

What is a Gecko?

The gecko, a member of the reptile family, is a lizard. It is small and scaly. Its body is covered with scales that change colour to mimic the surrounding environment. Although most geckos are nocturnal, some species are active during the day.

How Big is a Gecko?

A gecko's body can measure between ¾ inch and 16 inches long, depending on the species.

What Does a Gecko Eat?

Geckos eat insects.

Where do Geckos Live?

Geckos live in all warm and temperate zones on Earth. They are especially prevalent in regions of Central and South America, Africa, Australia, and the Mediterranean, and in the southern part of Asia.

Interesting Fact:

To catch prey, geckos can stay motionless for several minutes. When the prey comes close, the gecko will suddenly attack with a quick snap.

Interesting Skills:

Geckos can climb wherever they want. Their toes have fleshy pads on the tips that will stick to anything – even smooth walls. At night, they like to stay close to a light so that they can feed on insects that are attracted to it.

Do You Know?

The gecko is considered a domesticated animal because it can be raised in a terrarium. The terrarium needs to have light to provide warmth. It also should have a hiding place, so that the gecko feels safe. Don't forget a small bowl of water and some insects for the gecko to eat.

Can Anything Else Go Wrong?

Spike was tickling me and I couldn't stop squirming around. The gecko jumped off my elbow, **ZOOMED** across the room, and jumped out a window. The students all screamed! That's when the classroom door opened.

Miss Angel Paws walked in, followed by four other rodents. They looked as though they were also there for **Career Day**. As soon as the teacher came into the room, the entire class quietened down. She gave me a long look, and I turned red with embarrassment.

Antonia's eyes welled up with tears. "Spike ran away," she sobbed. "He's gone away forever!"

"Don't worry, we'll find him later," said Miss Angel Paws. "Now I want to introduce you to our other guests: Professor Sandsnout, RENOWNED EGYPTOLOGIST; Miss Lulu Soufflé, inventor of small-holed Swiss cheese; Professor Miles Magmamouse, volcanologist; and the world-famouse actor Robert Rodentford."

On hearing that name, the class clapped enthusiastically.

CAREER DAY

FIRST NAME: Cyril T.
LAST NAME: Sandsnout
NICKNAME: The Desert Rat
PROFESSION: Egyptologist
HIS HOBBY: He has an incredible collection of joke books. He loves to tell jokes and to play pranks, too!

FIRST NAME: Miles
LAST NAME: Magmamouse
NICKNAME: Lava Lover
PROFESSION: Volcanologist
HIS HOBBY: Ever since he was a little mouseling, he has always loved doing experiments. However, he has almost set his lab on fire on more than one occasion.

FIRST NAME: Lulu
LAST NAME: Soufflé
NICKNAME: Gouda
PROFESSION: Chef
HER HOBBY: Making cheese! She has invented many mouth-watering new cheeses, including her famouse small-holed Swiss cheese.

FIRST NAME: Robert
LAST NAME: Rodentford
NICKNAME: Blondie
PROFESSION: Actor
HIS HOBBY: He loves nature and animals, and has ten dogs! Horses run wild on his ranch.

Help! A Mummy!

Miss Angel Paws asked Professor Sandsnout, one of my dear old friends, to speak to the class. He immediately started talking about his work.

"Students, I'm an Egyp-tol-o-gist. That means I'm an expert on ANCIENT EGYPT. I'm also the director of the Egyptian Mouseum in New Mouse City. Have any of you ever visited the mouseum?"

There was a chorus of mouselings all shouting, **"I HAVE! I HAVE!"**

Just thinking about that mouseum made me shiver. I'm **TERRIFIED** of sarcophagi and I'm especially scared of mummies! (Don't tell anyone, but that mouseum gives me **NIGHTMARES**!)

Professor Sandsnout proudly placed a mysterious, old wooden sarcophagus on the desk. It was shaped like a cat.

"Oooooooooooooh!" said the class.

The lid looked heavy. Professor Sandsnout lifted it with both hands. Creeeeeak!

"Aaaaaaaaaaaaaah!" sighed the class.

Suddenly, the lid slipped from Professor Sandsnout's fingers. Bang!

"Yeee-oooow!" I screeched.

The lid had fallen on my paw!

This day was beyond bad!

When the professor began to pick up the sarcophagus lid, I quickly moved away, just in case.

That's when I saw Spike.

I tried to grab him, but he skittered through my legs, ran around the room, and climbed straight up the wall!

Knowing I couldn't catch Spike, I turned back to Professor Sandsnout. He had put something new on the desk – a **CAT MUMMY**!

"**Aaaack!**" I screeched. There's only one thing that scares me more than mummies, and it's cats!

I felt dizzy. I backed away. I tried to find something to grab on to. I didn't want to faint in front of the class! I felt a hand and I reached for it. But it wasn't someone's hand, it was a bone. In fact, it was a PILE OF BONES!

"**Aaaack!**" I screeched again.

I was so terrified, I almost ran out the door. Suddenly, my friend Professor Sandsnout grabbed me by the collar.

"Geronimo, where are you going?" he asked. "This guy's been dead for thousands of years! He's not going to hurt you!"

Well, I never said I wasn't a 'fraidy mouse.

MUMMIES

The Ancient Egyptians believed in life after death. When a person died, they preserved the body and its internal organs for the trip to the afterlife. To preserve the body, they used a technique called mummification.

HOW WERE MUMMIES MADE?

Mummification was a very long and detailed process that took seventy days. First, all the internal organs except the heart were removed and placed inside special containers called canopic jars. The heart was left inside the body. Then, to dry the body, the skin was covered with a special salt called natron. Next the sunken body was filled with linen, oil, and aromatic herbs to make it appear lifelike. Finally, it was wrapped in linen. Sometimes, a funeral mask was placed on the face of the mummy.

INTERESTING FACTS

The Ancient Egyptians worshipped many gods and goddesses. One was Bastet, the cat goddess. Egyptians believed cats were sacred. When cats died, they were mummified.

An Explosive Experiment

Luckily, Professor Sandsnout put the cat mummy and all those bones back into the sarcophagus. His talk was over. I sighed with relief. Now I could listen to the next guest, Professor Miles Magmamouse.

Professor Magmamouse lowered the blinds and put on a video that explained everything any mouse would ever want to know about **VOLCANOES**, volcanic ERUPTIONS, and earthquakes.

What an exciting line of work!

He had seen hundreds of volcanoes and lots of lava in his life.

Suddenly, my job seemed wimpy and boring. At some point, Professor Magmamouse asked me to give him a hand with the experiment. I listened closely because I didn't want to mess up. **I had to look good for Benjamin!**

"Geronimo, when I say NOW, put three drops of vinegar into the mouth of the volcano," Professor Magmamouse told me. "It is important you only add three drops. Is that clear?"

At that moment, my nose began to itch. I tried to hold my breath, but I couldn't stop myself from sneezing.

"AAAAchoooo!"

And that's how I poured the entire bottle of vinegar into the volcano. It erupted, and lava **OOZED** everywhere! What a mess!

Luckily, **HENRY HANDIPAWS**, the caretaker, arrived at once. He had a huge pail of cleaning supplies. He gave me one look and pulled out his biggest broom.

"Some people would blow their top over a mess like this," Henry commented. "But don't worry, Mr. Stilton, I'll get you squeaky clean in no time! You want to look EXTRA SPIFFY today." **Then he winked at me.**

MAKE A VOLCANIC ERUPTION WITH MILES MAGMAMOUSE!

WHAT YOU'LL NEED:

- 500 ml plastic bottle
- cardboard base, approximately three feet by three feet
- glue
- brown modelling clay (enough to sculpt a mountain)
- warm water
- baking soda
- washing-up liquid
- red food colouring (optional)
- a funnel
- vinegar

WHAT YOU'LL DO:

Be sure to ask an adult for help before you begin. To limit the mess, make your volcano outside or on a large table with a protective covering.

1. Glue the plastic bottle to the centre of the cardboard base.
2. Mould the brown modelling clay around the bottle to form a volcano.
3. Mix ½ cup water, ¼ cup baking soda, and one spoonful of liquid dish soap together. Use the funnel to help you pour the mixture into the bottle, which will become the mouth of your volcano. Add three drops of food colouring if desired.
4. Add three drops of vinegar to the mouth of the volcano, and enjoy the eruption!

When the baking soda mixes with the vinegar, it forms a foam that looks just like the lava in a volcanic eruption.

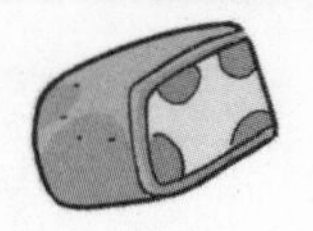

Cheese Tasting!

Mr. Handipaws finished cleaning me off just in time for me to hear Lulu Soufflé's presentation.

She was such a fascinating rodent. Her skin was as pale as mozzarella. Her hair was long and silky.

I could not take my eyes – or ears – off her.

Lulu was telling the class that she hadn't been a great student.

"When I was a little mouseling, my favourite subject in school was lunch," she said. "Nothing made me happier than **MUNCHING** on a piece of perfectly aged cheese. That's why I decided to make food my profession."

She knew **everything** about cheese. Lulu was sharper than New Mouse-style Cheddar.

LULU'S EASY CHEESY PIZZA FONDUE

BEFORE YOU BEGIN, ASK AN ADULT FOR HELP.

WHAT YOU'LL NEED:

1 750g jar pasta sauce (without meat)
450g grated mozzarella cheese
25g grated Parmesan cheese
2 teaspoons dried oregano
1 teaspoon garlic pepper
½ teaspoon onion powder
1 loaf French or Italian bread, cut into cubes

WHAT YOU'LL DO:

1. In a large pot or a slow cooker, combine the pasta sauce, cheeses, and spices.
2. Cook until cheese is melted and sauce is hot.
3. Be careful not to let it burn around the edges.
4. To eat, dip bread cubes in fondue and enjoy!

I could have listened to her all day. After all, cheese is one of my favourite subjects, especially when I'm hungry!

The best part of the presentation was when Lulu declared that she had talked enough. "Tasting is believing, so let's have a snack," she announced.

She lifted up a platter of all kinds of cheeses. Yum, yum! I picked an **ENORMOUSE** piece of cheese that had a funny smell and a greenish-blue colour. I was about to wolf it down when Lulu spoke.

"See, Mr. Stilton is about to taste a piece of blue cheese that is made from a special kind of mould –"

"MOULD????" I asked, quickly pulling the cheese away from my snout.

She smiled. "Of course," she said. "To make blue cheese, you use milk, milk enzymes, and moulds like these."

She placed a little bottle of greenish, bluish, VILE-SMELLING substance right under my nose.

The aroma was so **disgusting** that I turned greenish blue, then white, and then I fainted!

When I came to, Lulu seemed very concerned.

"I'm surprised you have such a weak stomach, Mr. Stilton," she said. "I really thought you were a mouse of great courage. And to think that I wanted you to help me cook my **triple-decker, super-duper cheese sandwiches** for everyone's lunch!"

I didn't want her to think I was a wimp. I jumped up.

"Not at all, Miss Lulu. Please, let me help you!"

But then I caught another whiff of the mould and I fainted again! **How embarrassing!**

Miss Lulu's Speciality

This time, I came to with some help from Punk Rat. He emptied an entire vase of water from the teacher's desk right on my head!

Brrr! The water was freezing!

At least I was able to walk with Lulu to the school kitchen to help her make some of her famouse triple-decker cheese sandwiches.

I really wanted to make a good impression because:

1. I was hungry and I wanted to sample some non-mouldy cheese.

2. Lulu was very *charming* and I never refuse to help a kind rodent, especially one who is so cute!

3. **Did I mention I was hungry?** I had to eat something, or else I would faint ... again!

Sadly, sneaking a treat was not so easy. I tried dipping

my paw into the cheese sauce, but Lulu caught me.

"I thought you had better manners, Mr. Stilton!" she scolded. "You should never sample a recipe until the cook says it's ready. **IT'S RUDE!**"

I became pink with embarrassment and didn't dare taste anything else, even as I made 757 triple-decker sandwiches.

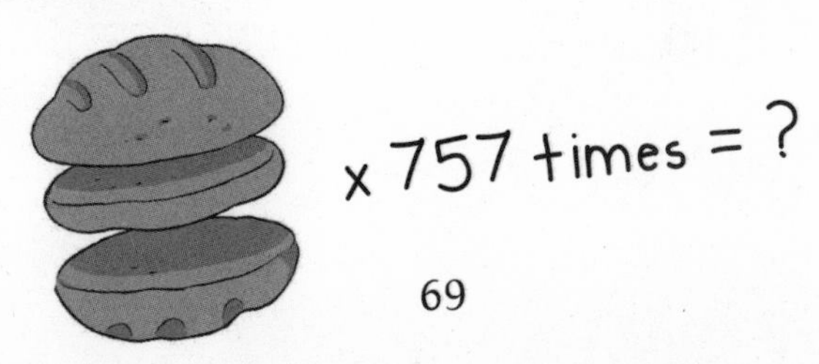

Every sandwich had three layers. I spread each layer of bread with Lulu's **DELICIOUS** special cheese sauce.

Go ahead, you tell me how many slices of bread I spread in total. I was never good at maths.

Then I cut 757 slices of turkey, and topped each sandwich with a cherry tomato, an olive, and a little New Mouse City flag. And I did that 757 times! And did I say how many times I accidentally stuck my paws with toothpicks? 359!

As soon as we finished the sandwiches, we took them to the canteen for our **RAVENOUS MOUSELINGS**. Of course, the food was a great success.

The sandwiches were so good that when it was my turn to serve myself, there were only crumbs left on the tray. I was so frustrated, I wanted to scream! I was sooooo hungry, I could have eaten the toothpicks!

Because Lulu was looking at me, I acted like nothing was wrong. **I had made a fool of myself enough already.**

GERONIMO'S GRILLED CHEESE MASTERPIECE

I'm no chef, but I made my own version of Lulu's sandwich at home. Ask an adult to help you make this cheeserific treat. It's super tasty! Yum!

WHAT YOU'LL NEED:

- butter
- two slices bread (not too thick!)
- three slices cheese (any combination of mozzarella, Cheddar, Gouda, Gruyere, Red Leicester, or Edam)
- smoked sliced turkey (one slice)
- pepperoni (four small slices)

WHAT YOU'LL DO:

1. Spread butter on one side of each slice of bread.
2. With an adult's help, place a frying pan over medium-low heat. Put one slice of bread in the frying pan, butter side down.
3. Place two pieces of cheese on top of the bread. Next add the turkey and pepperoni, and then the final piece of cheese. Place the second piece of bread, butter side up, on top.
4. When the cheese starts to melt and the bottom piece of bread turns golden brown, flip the sandwich with a spatula. When the second piece of bread is golden brown, it's done!

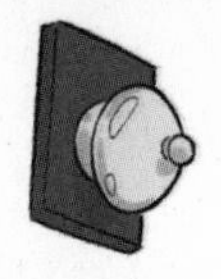

PLEASE, UNTANGLE MY PAWS!

After lunch (what lunch? I hadn't eaten anything. Sigh!), Benjamin and his friends had break time while the adults cleaned up the canteen.

I finished washing the dishes, and the boy did I need rest! That's when I heard that same familiar voice over the loudspeaker: **RINGGG!**

"Miss Angel Paws, please report to the principal's office right away."

I was sure I recognised that voice. **Where, oh where, had I heard it before?**

Miss Angel Paws asked me to sub for her again.

"Geronimo, would you please keep an eye on the **MOUSELINGS ON THE PLAYGROUND**?"

I wanted to ask: "Why me?! Why not Robert Rodentford, who's been sitting there sunning himself for the last hour while I made the lunch, served the meal, and scoured the tables???"

But Miss Angel Paws was already gone, and I had to:

1. Rescue one mouseling who was about to fall from a swing. (I barely caught him!)

2. Referee two basketball and three volleyball games. (My cheeks were weak from whistling!)

3. Break up four fights, clean five skinned snouts, and put plasters on six knees.

4. Place ice packs on seven lumps of various sizes and in various locations.

5. Dry the tears of eight little mice, and comfort nine mouselings with broken hearts. (I had to wring out my handkerchief after all those tears!)

And then Punk Rat challenged me to a race on the playground equipment. I was about to refuse, but suddenly Benjamin piped up.

"That's baby stuff for my uncle," Benjamin announced proudly. "He's not a wimp!"

After that statement, how could I say no? I climbed up the monkey bars and dove headfirst down the tunnel slide. All at once, I stopped. **I WAS STUCK!** I was too big for the slide!

I felt so sorry for myself. It was definitely a BAD day.

"Would somebody please get me out?!" I yelled.

DEFINITELY A BAD DAY

4.

There you go!

5.

I'm exhausted!

6.

WHAT ARE YOU DOING HERE?

Luckily, Henry Handipaws came to my rescue again. "Mr. Stilton, you've got yourself in a **tight squeeze**!" he said. He yanked me right out. What a close call! Henry patted me on the back and went on his way.

When we got to the classroom, *Miss Angel Paws* greeted me with a smile. She asked everyone to take a seat to listen to the next guest: the famouse actor Robert Rodentford.

I rolled my eyes. I was sure he'd talk about his blockbuster movies and his yacht and all the *beautiful rodents* who are in love with him. In other words, I had a preconceived* idea that he was a snobby and silly mouse.

*TO PRECONCEIVE IS TO FORM AN OPINION (THAT MAY NOT BE CORRECT) ABOUT SOMETHING OR SOMEONE BEFORE HAVING ALL THE FACTS.

I was wrong. He was much more than a handsome snout!

Robert Rodentford talked about the volunteer work he does to help **SAVE THE ENVIRONMENT**. In fact, he never talked about himself. He discussed all the ways a rodent can help protect the earth.

I knew immediately that we would be fast friends. We were very different, but we both cared about the same things.

I was very interested in what he had to say, but then I saw something **slink** by me. Sure enough, it was that sneaky, scaly class pet – Spike!

My entire family had begged me not to get into any trouble, not to make a fool of myself, and not to disappoint Benjamin. But that pesky gecko had got loose on my watch, and I felt responsible!

ROBERT RODENTFORD'S WORK TO SAVE THE ENVIRONMENT

MOUSEWEEK

OIL SPILL ENDANGERS PENGUINS

Robert Rodentford arrives to help after an oil tanker sinks and endangers penguins.

WHISKER ENQUIRER

WARNING: LARGE CITIES POLLUTED

Rodentford squeaks out about smog: the dark truth about a growing pollution problem on Mouse Island.

Rodentford helps sandbag city dams when there is a flood emergency in New Mousiana.

GORGONZOLA GAZETTE

GARBAGE GRIEF

Rodentford is down in the dumps about rubbish troubles.

I looked at Spike, and he seemed to be **smirking** at me. A second later, he SCURRIED across the room. Then he climbed the wall and **slipped** into the air-conditioning duct!

I decided to follow him. I just *had* to catch him! I had to do it for Benjamin.

So, I pulled myself into the dark duct. I followed Spike along the narrow passageway, above classrooms, under the gym, and into the cellar, until he headed out into the hallway. I was still on my paws and knees when I bumped into her: a *classy, refined* rodent with her fur pulled into a neat bun.

I looked at her, and she looked at me.

We both yelled at the same time: **"WHAT ARE YOU DOING HERE?"**

She had changed so much, but I knew it was her right away. How could I forget her?

It was *Veronica Stiffwhiskers*, my greatest rival during my school days! This was the mouse who had been so cute, so perfect, and **so great at everything**!

It had been her voice on the loudspeaker! She was now the principal of the school!

I was **dumbfounded**. I was trying to think of something intelligent to say when Spike scurried into an air-conditioning vent again. I mumbled a **SILLY excuse** and dove in after Spike.

I always made a fool of myself in front of Veronica.

As I was scampering after Spike in the duct, I thought, *I'm sure she thinks I grew up to be a big fool. Sigh!*

An (Almost) Olympic Performance

On all fours, I fumbled down the long duct, which was as dark as the belly of a **RAVENOUS CAT**.

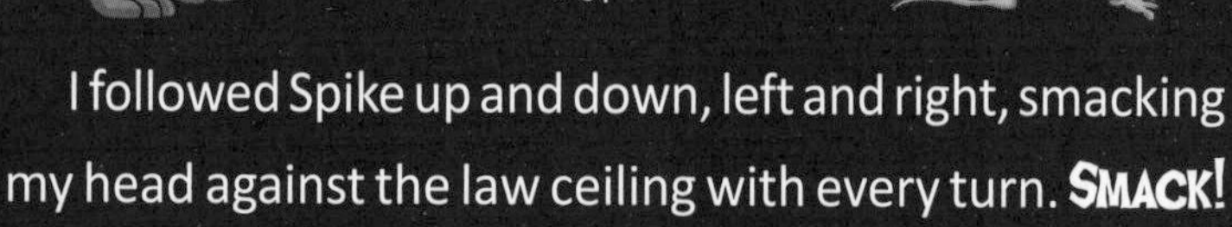

I followed Spike up and down, left and right, smacking my head against the law ceiling with every turn. **SMACK!**

Spike made a quick turn and was about to slip into a new grate.

I lunged forwards and pounced on him. All at once, I heard a creaking sound.

I fell,

fell,

fell,

fell,

down!

I made a triple somersault with an elegant twist, landing on my feet with slightly bent knees. My gymnastic form was *perfect*! I didn't do it on purpose. In fact, if I had tried to do it, there was no way I could have performed so well. It was an (almost) Olympic performance! But, of course, the one time I showed some agility and athletic ability, there was no one there to see me! Today had been full of so many blunders, I would have loved it if someone had seen my ***one shining moment***!

As I was thinking this, a floodlight blinded me and thunderous applause shook the walls. A chorus of voices yelled: **"Hooray for Geronimo!"**

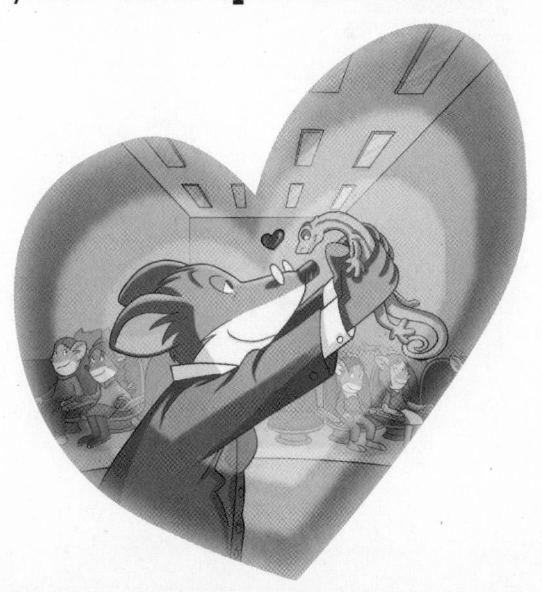

Stilton, Geronimo Stilton!

I was shocked!

Were they really all shouting my name?

"GE-RO-NI-MO! GE-RO-NI-MO! GE-RO-NI-MO! GE-RO-NI-MO!"

Was that *my* name on posters, programmes, and banners?

I rubbed my eyes. Maybe I had hit my head one too many times today. Maybe I had fainted.

I looked again. It was real. Everything was real. I wasn't dreaming. **HOLEY CHEESE!**

All these people were here for me. Veronica Stiffwhiskers came towards me with a huge smile. My, how she had changed!

"Today, on our school's **Career Day**, we want to

honour our most famouse graduate. He's a wonderful example of how great achievement is possible through working hard every day and really loving what you do. He's won a RATITZER PRIZE for his scoop on *The Curse of the Cheese Pyramid*, and he is a bestselling writer. His name is Stilton, *Geronimo Stilton*!"

Thunderous applause erupted around me.

Among the cheering audience, I saw my family standing to the side. No one was missing. Benjamin, Thea, Trap, Grandfather William, Aunt Sweetfur ... all of the Stiltons were there.

And there was Petunia Pretty Paws!

The principal's voice shook me back to reality.

"... and to properly honour Little Tails Academy's *most famouse graduate*, who is also a dear old friend, I'd like to present him with a plaque to remember this day."

While the photographers were shooting a million photos and the FLASHES were blinding me, she handed me a beautiful plaque engraved with my name.

"And if Geronimo Stilton doesn't mind, we'd like to keep the plaque in the school's lobby. It would be an honour to show it in our trophy case, next to the medals, plaques, and trophies that our students have won."

Then she winked at me.

My, how she had changed!

More photos! How embarrassing!

PHOTOS AND AUTOGRAPHS

SO MANY PHOTOGRAPHERS!

HELP! THE FLASHES ARE BLINDING ME!

MORE PHOTOS! HOW EMBARRASSING!

HERE IS MY AUTOGRAPH!

WHAT AN HONOUR!

THANK YOU, EVERYONE.
I'M VERY TOUCHED!

Top-Notch Nibbles for Cheese-Loving Mice!

Once the ceremony was over, the principal invited us to the dining hall. A **fabumouse** buffet had been set up, and there were countless cheesy delicacies!

There was a plate of Lulu's famouse triple-decker cheese sandwiches, along with many other amazing

snacks: fondue, blue cheese mousse tarts, mozzarella and Cheddar cheese, cheese shish-kebabs, and Swiss cheese soufflé. Lulu had organised the buffet and, I can assure you, I have never seen more **SCRUMPTIOUS**, divine, original, *whisker-licking delicacies* in my life!

In other words, they were top-notch nibbles for cheese-loving mice! It was then that I remembered that I hadn't eaten breakfast or lunch. **I was absolutely famished!**

I was about to throw myself at the buffet when someone tapped me on the shoulder.

TAP, TAP!

I turned and saw a long, long line of rodents of every age waiting to congratulate me. I put down my sandwich with a sigh and turned towards them. I realised I would be skipping yet another meal. When I saw the first rodent in line was Henry Handipaws, I forgot my **RAVENOUS** hunger.

"Thanks to you, I didn't make a complete fool of myself today," I told him warmly.

Suddenly, another rodent jumped out from behind him. **They were almost identical!**

"Geronimo Stilton, you never change," the second mouse exclaimed. "You still get into such trouble!"

I stared at both of them, dumbfounded.

The second mouse's whiskers were greyer, he wasn't wearing a uniform, and he had a bit of a tummy, but otherwise the two mice almost looked like mirror images!

It was the legendary **HAVARTI HANDIPAWS**. He had been the caretaker during my time at Little Tails Academy. Back then, he helped me get out of tight squeezes a million times a day!

Henry Handipaws smiled.

"LIKE FATHER, LIKE SON!" he said. "Now you know why I knew so much about you, Mr. Stilton. My father told so many stories about you, and I decided to do the same kind of work as my father. I wanted to help a lot of shy little mice have more confidence in themselves."

I thanked them both from the bottom of my heart and spent the rest of the afternoon shaking hands, smiling, and signing autographs.

After half an hour, my paw was weak from all the handshakes. After an hour, my cheeks were numb from smiling so much. And after two hours, my shoulders were bruised from all the slaps and pats on the back!

But I was happy. Very, very happy.

I was actually ecstatic!

Now I'm in There, Too!

Even Grandfather William congratulated me. He slapped me on the shoulder the hardest!

"Good for you, Grandson!" he bellowed as I staggered from the blow to my shoulder. "This time you seemed like an **UPSTANDING** mouse."

Trap threw a spitball in my ear.

"Nice going, Cousin," he said. "You looked less of a fool than usual. Except when you fell from the ceiling, that is!"

Aunt Sweetfur was worried about me. "You're pale," she whispered. "**DIDN'T YOU EAT ENOUGH?**"

She placed a sweet little cheese tart in my paw. I stuffed it in my mouth before somebody could prevent me from tasting that little bit of heaven. It was deeelicious!

Robert Rodentford, Professor Sandsnout, Lulu Soufflé, Professor Magmamouse, and many other friends came over to **CONGRATULATE** me.

My friend Petunia Pretty Paws came over to give me a tiny kiss on the tip of my whiskers.

"I'm proud of you, Geronimo!" she said.

I was so embarrassed, I turned as red as a tomato. Luckily, Benjamin came to give me a high five that almost took off my paw!

"You're awesome, Uncle Geronimo!" he exclaimed.

Behind him were all his school friends. Antonia had Spike in her arms.

"HOORAY FOR GERONIMO!" they all yelled at once.

"HIP, HIP, HOORAY FOR SPIKE'S HERO!"

"Tell me, Geronimo, did you like the surprise?" Veronica Stiffwhiskers asked.

Then she turned to the mouselings.

"Hurry, everyone head to the reception," she instructed them. "We have one more VERY IMPORTANT thing we need to do!"

The mouselings happily accompanied me to the reception. Veronica winked at me as she opened the trophy case.

"This time, you win!" she said. "You're our most famouse graduate."

She placed the plaque with my name on it inside the case.

"Thank you!" I shouted happily. "Now I'm in there, too!"

THE RODENT'S GAZETTE

1. Main entrance
2. Printing presses (where everything is printed)
3. Accounts department
4. Editorial room (where editors, illustrators, and designers work)
5. Geronimo Stilton's office
6. Geronimo's botanical garden

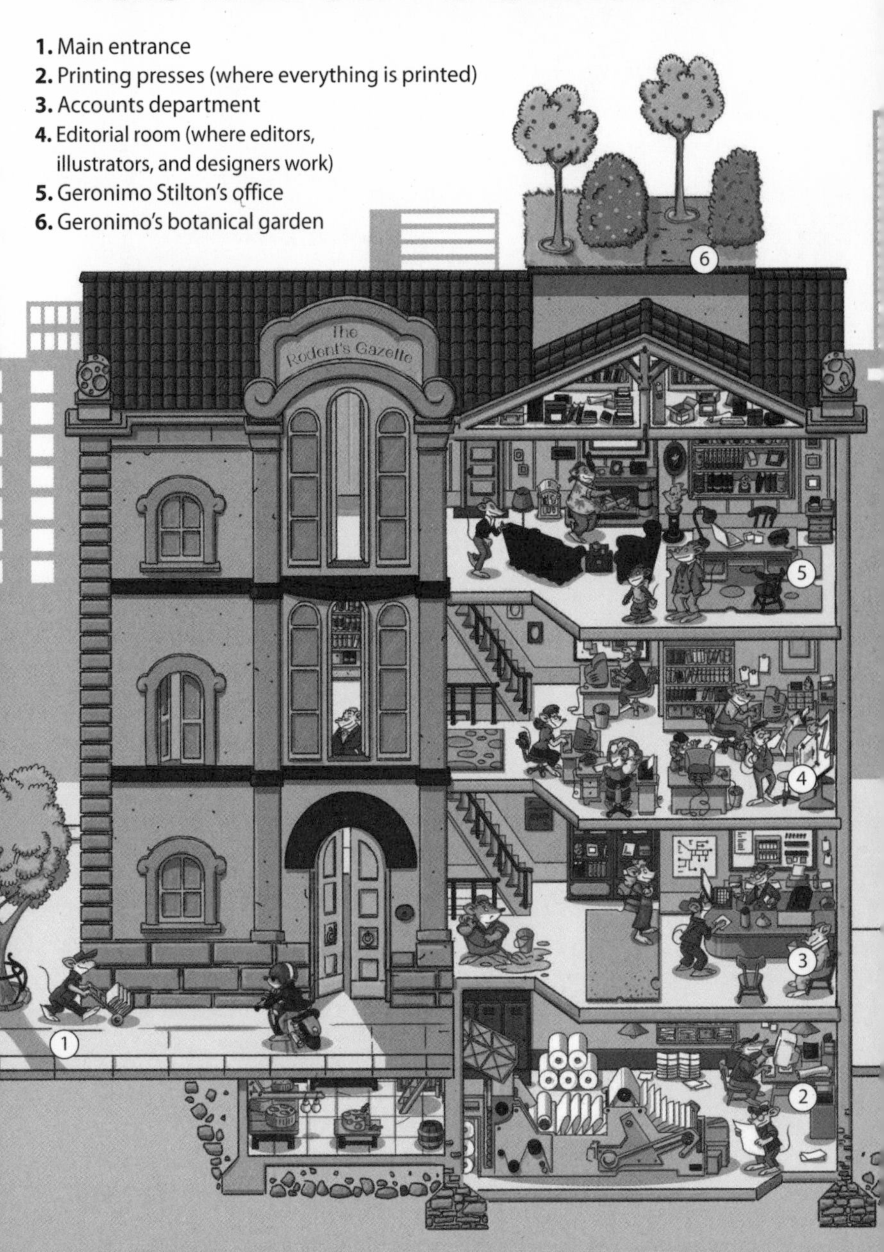

9
1
18
2
4
8
3
12
32
13
11
19
10
22
5
46
45
20
15
17
7
40
24
26
25
28
33
14
16
38
27
36
23
37
31
21
29
35
44
41
30
34
6
42
39
43

MAP OF NEW MOUSE CITY

1. Industrial Zone
2. Cheese Factories
3. Angorat International Airport
4. WRAT Radio and Television Station
5. Cheese Market
6. Fish Market
7. Town Hall
8. Snotnose Castle
9. The Seven Hills of Mouse Island
10. Mouse Central Station
11. Trade Centre
12. Movie Theatre
13. Gym
14. Catnegie Hall
15. Singing Stone Plaza
16. The Gouda Theatre
17. Grand Hotel
18. Mouse General Hospital
19. Botanical Gardens
20. Cheap Junk for Less (Trap's store)
21. Parking Lot
22. Mouseum of Modern Art
23. University and Library
24. The Daily Rat
25. The Rodent's Gazette
26. Trap's House
27. Fashion District
28. The Mouse House Restaurant
29. Environmental Protection Centre
30. Harbour Office
31. Mousidon Square Garden
32. Golf Course
33. Swimming Pool
34. Blushing Meadow Tennis Courts
35. Curlyfur Island Amusement Park
36. Geronimo's House
37. Historic District
38. Public Library
39. Shipyard
40. Thea's House
41. New Mouse Harbour
42. Luna Lighthouse
43. The Statue of Liberty
44. Hercule Poirat's Office
45. Petunia Pretty Paws's House
46. Grandfather William's House

MAP OF MOUSE ISLAND

1. Big Ice Lake
2. Frozen Fur Peak
3. Slipperyslopes Glacier
4. Coldcreeps Peak
5. Ratzikistan
6. Transratania
7. Mount Vamp
8. Roastedrat Volcano
9. Brimstone Lake
10. Poopedcat Pass
11. Stinko Peak
12. Dark Forest
13. Vain Vampires Valley
14. Goosebumps Gorge
15. The Shadow Line Pass
16. Penny-Pincher Castle
17. Nature Reserve Park
18. Las Ratayas Marinas
19. Fossil Forest
20. Lake Lake
21. Lake Lakelake
22. Lake Lakelakelake
23. Cheddar Crag
24. Cannycat Castle
25. Valley of the Giant Sequoia
26. Cheddar Springs
27. Sulphurous Swamp
28. Old Reliable Geyser
29. Vole Vale
30. Ravingrat Ravine
31. Gnat Marshes
32. Munster Highlands
33. Mousehara Desert
34. Oasis of the Sweaty Camel
35. Cabbagehead Hill
36. Rattytrap Jungle
37. Rio Mosquito
38. Mousefort Beach
39. San Mouscisco
40. Swissville
41. Cheddarton
42. Mouseport
43. New Mouse City
44. Pirate Ship of Cats

4
3
2
44
1
7
6
5
40
14
8
13
25
9
11
12
41
10
42
21
15
22
20
39
23
17
32
16
19
26
35
18
29
24
43
28
38
30
27
36
31
33
37
34

THE COLLECTION

HAVE YOU READ ALL OF GERONIMO'S ADVENTURES?

- ☐ *Lost Treasure of the Emerald Eye*
- ☐ *The Curse of the Cheese Pyramid*
- ☐ *Cat and Mouse in a Haunted House*
- ☐ *I'm Too Fond of My Fur!*
- ☐ *Four Mice Deep in the Jungle*
- ☐ *Paws Off, Cheddarface!*
- ☐ *Fangs and Feasts in Transratania*
- ☐ *Attack of the Pirate Cats*

- ☐ *A Fabumouse Holiday for Geronimo*
- ☐ *Hang on to Your Whiskers*
- ☐ *School Trip to Niagara Falls*
- ☐ *The Christmas Toy Factory*
- ☐ *Geronimo Stilton, Secret Agent*
- ☐ *A Fantastic School Adventure*
- ☐ *The Cheese Experiment*
- ☐ *The Super Chef Contest*
- ☐ *Welcome to Mouldy Manor*
- ☐ *The Treasure of Easter Island*
- ☐ *Mouse Overboard!*
- ☐ *This Hotel Is Haunted*

ABOUT THE AUTHOR

Born in New Mouse City, Mouse Island, GERONIMO STILTON is Rattus Emeritus of Mousomorphic Literature and of Neo-Ratonic Comparative Philosophy. For the past twenty years, he has been running The Rodent's Gazette, New Mouse City's most widely read daily newspaper.

Stilton was awarded the Ratitzer Prize for his scoops on *The Curse of the Cheese Pyramid* and *The Search for Sunken Treasure*. He has also received the Andersen Prize for Personality of the Year. His works have been published all over the globe.

In his spare time, Mr. Stilton collects antique cheese rinds and plays golf. But what he most enjoys is telling stories to his nephew Benjamin.